For Jenny
—N. B.

For the kind people at Villa Montessori
—G. B. K.

HarperCollins®, 🎬®, I Can Read Book®, and Harper Trophy® are
trademarks of HarperCollins Publishers Inc.

Sid and Sam
Copyright © 1996 by Nola Buck
Illustrations copyright © 1996 by G. Brian Karas
Printed in the U.S.A. All rights reserved.

Library of Congress Cataloging-in-Publication Data
Buck, Nola.
    Sid and Sam / by Nola Buck ; illustrated by G. Brian Karas.
        p.   cm. — (My first I can read book)
    Summary: Sid sings a long song that drives Sam crazy.
    ISBN 0 06-025371-1. — ISBN 0-06-025372-X (lib. bdg.)
    ISBN 0-06-444211-X (pbk.)

    [1. Singing—Fiction.]   I. Karas, G. Brian, ill   II. Title.   II. Series.
PZ7.B878Si   1996   94-36/11
[E]—dc20   CIP
                                                                                    AC

❖
First Trophy edition, 1997

Visit us on the World Wide Web!
http://www.harperchildrens.com

MY FIRST
I Can Read Book®

Sid and Sam

by Nola Buck
pictures by G. Brian Karas

Harper Trophy®
A Division of HarperCollins *Publishers*

Sid saw Sam.

Sam saw Sid.

"Please sing," said Sid.
"Sing a song, Sam."

"Sure thing," said Sam.
"I will sing."

Sam sang.

Sam sang a long song.

Sid sang along with Sam.

"Sing slower, Sid," Sam said.

Sid sang slower.

"Sing softer, Sid," Sam said.

Sid sang softer.

"Sing lower, Sid," Sam said.

Sid sang lower.

Sid sang low.

Sid sang so low.

"Stop, Sid.

Please stop," Sam said.

"Sure, Sam," said Sid.

"I will stop."

"Soon, Sid?" Sam said.

"Soon?"

"Soon, Sam," Sid said.
"Soon."

Sid sang a new song.

Sid sang, and sang,
and sang.

"Sid," Sam said.

"That song is so long."

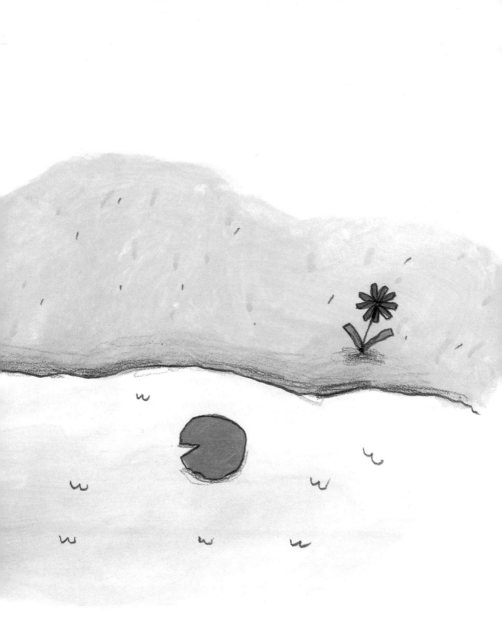

"So long?" said Sid.

"So long," Sam said.

"So long, Sid!"

"See you soon!"